Bim and Bom
A Shabbat Tale

This
PJ BOOK
belongs to

_____

_____

PjLibrary®

JEWISH BEDTIME STORIES and SONGS

To the "tots" of Temple Israel, for getting me
started, to Leslie, for helping me along the
way, and to Roya for everything.
—DS

For The Egg Family with love.
—MI

KAR-BEN PUBLISHING, INC.
A division of Lerner Publishing Group
241 First Avenue North
Minneapolis, MN 55401 U.S.A.
1-800-4-Karben

Website address: www.karben.com

Library of Congress Cataloging-in-Publication Data

Swartz, Daniel J.
  Bim and Bom : a Shabbat tale / by Daniel J. Swartz ; illustrated by Melissa Iwai.
  – Rev. ed.
      p.   cm.
  Summary: Bim, a housebuilder, and Bom, a baker, work hard all week, and then
spend every Friday doing good deeds, "mitzvot," and meet joyfully at sundown to
celebrate Shabbat together.
  ISBN 978-0-7613-6717-8 (pbk. : alk. paper)
  [1. Sabbath—Fiction. 2. Judaism—Customs and practices—Fiction. 3. Jews—
Fiction.] I. Iwai, Melissa, ill. II. Title.
PZ7.S97336Bi 2011
[E]—dc22   2010028264

Manufactured in China
4-42262-11787-7/13/2016

011723.2K4/B0754/A3

Bim and Bom

A Shabbat Tale

by Daniel J. Swartz

illustrated by Melissa Iwai

KAR-BEN
PUBLISHING

BIM AND HER BROTHER BOM lived on opposite ends of town.

All week long they were busy working, and
they didn't get to see each other.

But on Shabbat, they could spend all day together.
So each week, they could hardly wait until it was
Shabbat again.

Bim was a carpenter, and she built the most wonderful houses in the whole town.

During the week she was busy building a new house for the mayor, or the grocer, or the rabbi. All day long she would work and work.

But Friday was different. Every Friday
Bim stopped working on the house she was
building. Instead, she spent Fridays building nice,
comfortable homes for people who couldn't afford
to pay her. By the time Shabbat arrived, she felt she
had done a mitzvah, a good deed.

Bim loved building, but Bom couldn't even build a
birdhouse. Every time he tried to build something,
he would hit his thumb with the hammer.

But Bom loved to bake, and he was the best baker in the
whole town. Everyone loved his bread and rolls and
muffins. He was busy all week baking bread for the
teacher, and the artist, and the gardener. All day
long he would knead dough for bread.

But Friday was different. Every Friday, he baked only challah, lots and lots of challah. He made the most beautiful challah that anyone had ever seen. It was light and sweet, with fancy braids and golden raisins. On Friday when Bom's challah was baking, the whole town smelled wonderful.

Bom knew that not everyone had enough money to buy challah for Shabbat, so he always made extra loaves and gave them to people who could not afford to pay him. By the time Shabbat came, he felt he had done a mitzvah, a good deed.

All Friday long, while Bim was building mitzvah houses, she would look out of the window to watch for the sun to set.

All Friday long, while Bom was baking mitzvah challah, he would listen to the clock in the bakery tick away, one hour, then another, then another.

When it was almost time to light the candles, Bim would put away her tools, wash her hands, brush her hair, and start running to Bom's end of town.

Bom would take off his apron and baker's hat, comb the flour out of his hair, and put a sign on his bakery window: *Closed for Shabbat*. He would start running to Bim's end of town.

They would run and run until, just at the same moment,
they would come to the square in the exact center of town.

Bim would shout, "Bom!"

Bom would shout, "Bim!"

And they would run to each other,
hug and say, "Shabbat shalom!"

Then they would
go off to Bim's nice,
comfortable house,
and celebrate
Shabbat with Bom's
delicious challah.

SHABBAT SHALOM

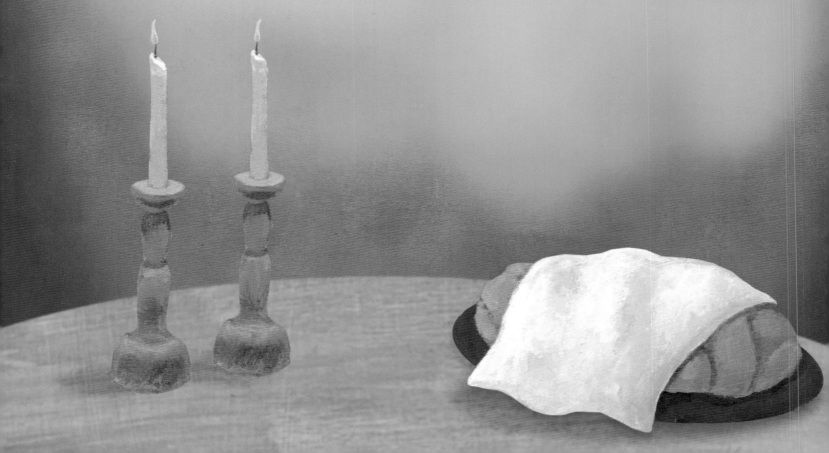